Stories of
WITCHES

Christopher Rawson
Adapted by Gill Harvey

Illustrated by
Stephen Cartwright

Reading Consultant: Alison Kelly
University of Surrey Roehampton

Contents

Chapter 1

The lost broomstick

This story begins with a witch called Bess and an invitation to a party. Bess loved parties. There was just one problem.

It's a long way away.

Bess couldn't remember where she had put her broomstick. She looked everywhere.

Boots... spare cauldron... hmmph. No broomstick.

But it was no good. The broomstick was lost. At last, Bess had to give up.

Now what could she do? She couldn't fly without her stick and it was too far to walk.

Then she had a great idea. "My magic rope!" she cried.

"I can turn someone into a horse and ride to the party. I just need to find someone."

Bess hid behind a tree and waited. Soon, a man came along. His wife walked behind him, carrying all their heavy bags.

Bess let the man pass. "He's no good, he's limping," she said. "Besides, his wife will be strong from carrying all those bags."

She jumped out and threw her rope over the woman.

At once, the woman turned into a horse. Bess climbed onto her back.

"Now for the party. Giddy-up!" she cried.

The man kept limping. At first, he didn't notice what had happened. But when he looked back...

...all he could see were his bags, and a horse galloping off in the distance.

The man went to get the bags, but he couldn't find his wife. Nobody had seen her.

Crossly, the man picked up the heavy bags. "I'll just have to carry these myself," he said.

A long way away Bess had stopped. The horse was worn out – and so were her shoes.

At the next village, Bess took her to a blacksmith. With four new horseshoes, the horse was ready to go.

At the party, the other witches pointed to the horse.

"Look at Bess without a broomstick!" they said and cackled with laughter.

Look, it's Bess on a horse. Ha, ha!

But Bess didn't mind. It was a wonderful party. The witches skipped around a cauldron, singing silly songs...

...before casting spells on each other, just for fun.

All too soon, the party was over. The other witches flew off on their broomsticks. Bess untied her horse and set out for home.

Fly safely!

Bess was nearly home when she met the man she had seen before. He was still carrying the heavy bags.

"Hello," she said. "Would you like to buy this horse? I don't need her anymore."

"What a good idea!" said
the man. "Then I won't have
to carry these bags. I lost my
wife, you see."

Bess said nothing. She
just smiled.

The man gave Bess a bag
of gold and climbed onto
the horse.

With the horse to carry him, the man was home in no time. He took the horse to a stable.

"What a fine beast you are," he said, patting her. He took off the rope...

...and jumped back with surprise. The horse had turned into his wife – just like that!

But...
but how?

She was pleased to see that being a horse hadn't changed her too much. But there was one difference...

...which meant she couldn't carry the bags anymore. From then on, every time they went shopping, her husband had to do it.

He kept asking her to turn back into a horse, just to show him the secret. She never did.

Chapter 2

Dog spell

Early one morning, Farmer Crumb and his wife set off to work in the fields. Their daughter Kate carried a picnic basket, full of food.

They worked hard all morning. Then Farmer Crumb looked up. "Time for lunch!" he said.

Kate ran off to the barn where she had hidden their picnic basket.

But before she reached the barn, Kate heard a strange sound. *Zzzzzzz*, it went. *Zzzzzzz…*

She peeked inside. An old witch was lying in the hay, fast asleep. And she'd found the picnic basket.

Kate was very angry. "How dare you!" she cried.

The witch woke up with a jump. Kate shouted at her some more.

You greedy old woman! We're hungry!

"How dare you speak to me like that," snarled the witch. "I'll teach you a lesson!"

Before Kate could move, the witch had cast a spell. "Maxi-baxi-jollybee-hog, get on the ground and bark like a dog!"

Poor Kate crawled back to her mother and father.

"Woof!" she barked. She couldn't say anything else.

"What happened?" cried her mother.

Look! A witch!

Hee hee heee!

Farmer Crumb chased after the witch. "Come back here!" he yelled. "What have you done to my daughter?"

Change her back, or I'll...

The witch just laughed. "You can't catch me!" she shouted, as she flew off on her broomstick.

Farmer Crumb and his wife took Kate home.

"What can we do?" they asked their friends. Mrs. Crumb was very upset.

But no one knew how to help.

"We must go to Rimpole," said Farmer Crumb, at last. Rimpole was an old wizard who lived on a hill. "If anyone can help us, he can."

Woof-woof!

She's done nothing but bark for three days!

Kate had to crawl to his house on her hands and knees. "Please help," begged her dad.

Rimpole frowned. "I can't break the spell," he said. "But I might be able to catch the witch for you."

He stared into his crystal ball. "Aba-doo-well! Who cast the spell?" he cried.

The witch's face appeared in the ball. "Ah, it's *you*, is it?" muttered Rimpole. "I might have known."

Rimpole fetched toadstools, nails, mustard powder and red berries. He mixed them and he pounded them. Then he added a splash of ketchup.

He heated the brew until
it bubbled gently. "Perfect!"
he said. He looked into his
crystal ball again.

But the witch wasn't
scared of anyone –
especially Rimpole.

As the brew began to bubble more fiercely, the wizard chanted a spell.

Tongues of fire, flames of might, give the nasty witch a fright!

At once, the cork flew out of the bottle and flames shot up the chimney.

That wiped the smile off the witch's face. She began to look very worried indeed.

She saw the flames creeping up on her. "Help!" she squealed and began to run...

But the flames were too
quick for her.

"Oh, stop them, stop them!"
cried the witch.

As soon as the witch made her promise, Kate jumped to her feet. She wasn't a dog anymore.

The family never saw the witch again. But, after that, Kate was always careful where she hid the picnic basket.

Chapter 3

The farmer's revenge

Farmer Jones had a big brown
cow. Every day, she gave
him five buckets full of the
creamiest milk in the village.

In the same village, there lived a greedy witch. She didn't have a cow, but she did love creamy milk.

One day, she had an idea for a wicked spell. "From now on, the milk will all be mine!" she cackled.

Next morning, Farmer Jones took the buckets of milk to his milk churn, as usual.

But as he poured it, he got a shock. The milk just disappeared. Not a drop was left.

Where's it gone?

Farmer Jones was furious.

"Calm down, dear," said his wife. "That won't bring the milk back. I'm sure we can find out what the problem is."

I'll soon sort this out!

And she set off for the village, to see what was going on.

The witch
was pumping
water at the
village pump.

"That's funny looking
water!" muttered Mrs. Jones.

The witch
filled her
bucket. She
walked off,
grinning.

The naughty witch hadn't pumped water at all.

"Aha!" cried Mrs. Jones and ran all the way home.

When she told her husband about the witch, he smiled.

"I know what to do," he said. "I have a sneaky plan."

This problem needs sorting out!

The next time he went to milk his cow, he took a big box with him.

He emptied the milk
into the churn. It
disappeared,
just as before.
But then
he did
something
else.

Ha-ha! See how
that tastes, witch!

He opened
the box and
tipped in
lots of white
powder, too.

In the village, the witch
filled her bucket with milk.
She dipped her mug into it.
"Lovely milk!" she cried,
and took a big gulp.

Clever,
clever me!

But the milk began to
bubble and froth. The witch
began to splutter and cough.
Farmer Jones had added soap
powder to it.

Soon, the witch was burping
bubbles. She had soapy
hiccups for a week – and she
never stole milk again.

Try these other books in
Series One:

Giants: Some giants are naughty,
some are foolish, but they're all
enormous. These stories tell how
a kind giant called a troll helped a
poor fisherman, and how three
wicked giants met a grisly end.

The Monster Gang: Starting
a gang is a great idea. So is
dressing up like monsters. But if
everyone is in disguise, how do
you know who's who?

Wizards: Here are three magical
tales about three very different
wizards. One is kind, one is clever
and one knows more secret spells
than the other two together.

Series editor: Lesley Sims

Designed by
Katarina Dragoslavić

This edition first published in 2002 by Usborne Publishing Ltd.,
Usborne House, 83-85 Saffron Hill, London EC1N 8RT, England.
www.usborne.com
Copyright © 2002, 1980 Usborne Publishing Ltd.